HOME

CC Stang

John, Karen ☺

Thank-you so much for
being such awesome RV
neighbors. Your kindness
and thoughtfulness is
so appreciated.

Enjoy!
(Rionaune

 FriesenPress

Suite 300 - 990 Fort St
Victoria, BC, V8V 3K2
Canada

www.friesenpress.com

ISBN
978-1-4602-9470-3 (Hardcover)
978-1-4602-9471-0 (Paperback)
978-1-4602-9472-7 (eBook)

1. FICTION, SHORT STORIES (SINGLE AUTHOR)

Distributed to the trade by The Ingram Book Company

List of Short Stories

Going Home

"Whispering Pines" — the melody and the words — played through Beth Ann's mind as she wandered through the forest. It was a meditative spot for her — a retreat really. She went there often, whether for moments of joy or for introspection. The forest nourished her restless spirit. On this day, she was choosing to recall that time — the one that over the years she often swallowed and couldn't view. But now the day had come to look headlong into that blessing.

The years had passed in some ways simply as a blink. Beth Ann had completed the necessary tasks. She recalled some enthusiasm and eagerness for many of her days and also moments of despair and tragedy that brought forth something in her she knew only at the soul level.

There was that time when Beth Ann was just starting grade school when her favourite teacher blessed her with kind praise and responsibility in the classroom. There was the cruel teacher who made her *stand* in the corner and pray Hail Marys. Oh, yes, and she recalled the great fun swimming at the river, working in the vegetable garden, and picking raspberries and saskatoons; the smells of summer and the beauty of winter; icicles dripping from the roof; the breathtaking beauty of horror frost on the trees; and ice skating on the river and snow shoeing in the forest. She remembered drinking snow water and using an outhouse, her mother kneading bread for their ever growing family, her father in the barn taking care of the livestock, and the family all sharing in endless household and farming chores.

Her parents shared music almost daily with the children, encouraging all to sing and play. Mother's piano playing and Father's booming baritone voice would ring through the small log cabin on many long winter evenings. So much of Beth Ann's life had been idyllic and simple, but a restlessness remained. She pondered this as she reflected back.

Beth Ann thought back to February 14, 1960: her 30th birthday and tenth wedding anniversary. The day dawned quite sparkly with the sun on the snow. She could hear her children stirring as she put the coffeepot on the stove to perk. She looked out the window at the embracing pines dusted with fresh snow and was looking forward to walking among them later. Her husband, George, had been out at the barn early as usual. He greeted her every day with a "Good morning, pretty lady. Join you for coffee in an hour or so."

Beth Ann knew George loved the early morning with the animals. It was his heaven. The children greeted Beth Ann with a big "Happy birthday!" and downed the hearty oatmeal with fresh cream, toast, and raspberry jam breakfast. Beth Ann smiled at the three wholesome faces: nine-year-old Jenny, seven-year-old Steve, and three-year-old Ezra. Beth Ann had had two miscarriages so she felt that these three would be all the children they would have. She instructed Jenny and Steve to bundle up and go tell their father his breakfast was ready and to collect the eggs from the chicken coop. The children did as asked and headed to the barn.

The rest of that day and for many after, Beth Ann felt as if she was in another reality for surely this couldn't be her life. Her children came running back saying their father was lying in the barn not moving. His heart had simply stopped and he went "home." Beth Ann's mind tried to make rational sense of this event, for although her husband was twenty years older than she, he was a fit man. It was simply too short a time for them to be together. They met when George was thirty-nine and she was nineteen. He was a hardworking farmer and very good man. Beth Ann was drawn to him in spite of the age difference. They married within four months of meeting and settled into their lives easily. How could she proceed now?

February 14, 1970, dawned, and, with ten years having passed, Beth Ann reflected on the direction her life had gone. Through the kindness of neighbours and hard work, she was able to proceed with some level of normalcy to her life. She sold the farm and bought a house in the town nearby. She was a gifted seamstress so was able to earn a good living in town for her family. Denim had come into style, and Beth Ann bought a heavy-duty machine so she was able to work with the fabric. Her natural ability meant she could fix, repair, or create whatever the project was. It brought her a measure of satisfaction.

The children were all in their teens now. Jenny loved nursing so had moved to the city for her formal training. The oil industry was getting going in their area, and Steve was already working hard at a roughneck job that took him to different locations often. Ezra wouldn't be far behind, and Beth Ann felt herself catch her breath. Over the years, she had often felt her husband by her side. When she despaired and the tears wouldn't stop, it was almost as if he was holding her once again. She was grateful for this, even though her heartache remained and she was unable to open her heart to any other man. The children brought great joy, and although she saw their grief at times, they were there for one another always. *What would life bring now?* she wondered.

February 14, 1980, was Beth Ann's fiftieth birthday. Her children had prospered and wanted to take her on a momentous trip — and they did. Coming from and living in a landlocked area, it was an extra-special treat to walk barefoot in the ocean, eat fresh clam chowder and fish, watch the sunset on the ocean, and share loving family moments. Beth

Ann felt inspired at the ocean and also felt a new measure of peace — one that had eluded her up until now. She inhaled the salt air deeply and released the tension within her body and mind. Her gaze fell gently on the water, and she felt a deep connection with herself for the first time in her life.

The vacation went by quickly, and the family were eager to get back to their busy lives. Jenny's nursing career was very satisfying to her, and marriage and children were right around the corner. Beth Ann was sewing Jenny's dress for the June wedding. Her heart was full creating the lovely gown for her daughter. Steve continued his lucrative work in the oil field and had been promoted throughout the years. He had already explored a lot of the world, and now his job would be taking him abroad as well. Ezra was still working on his law degree and entertained the family with his case study stories. That boy's sense of humour made for many moments of hilarity.

February 14, 1990, began with Beth Ann sleeping in. She awoke with a start. *Eight o'clock in the morning. Goodness, I'm always awake by six,* she thought. *Maybe now that I'm sixty, I'll become a sleepy head.* The thought amused her as she had been a morning person her whole life. The past ten years had brought such tender events and emotions to the family. Being grandma to three little girls opened Beth Ann's heart and allowed so much love to flow, even creating space for a companion in her life. Her friend, Jim, had brought a light to her eyes that had been dim for quite a while. He also brought new thoughts and ideas, helping Beth Ann to expand her awareness about this earthly existence. It was beginning to feel like the puzzle pieces were all going to fit. The restlessness was more intermittent now. She still loved to stitch and sew and create. Her children's lives, although very much their own, always found time and space for one another.

February 14, 2000, felt like an impossible date to Beth Ann. There had been so many dramatic changes in the world since her birth in 1930. From no electricity or running water or telephone in her rural youth to instant access to just about anything, including the world via the Internet. She had embraced the changes as a necessity in continuing with her business. The treadle sewing machine she learned to sew with had progressed to a computer model now, and, yes, it was convenient, but she still kept an older model and did some hand stitching for the pure pleasure of it. She noticed her eyesight changing the last few years, so she used eye glasses most of the time now. Time had marched on steadily, and she soldiered on with it.

Seventy years. Yes, there would be the cake and gathering and well-wishes today, and the family in the area would be stopping in. She had been talking with her three children over the last year about moving to a senior dwelling. Beth Ann was drawn to it as the location was very close to the home she and George had shared. It was no longer a rural area because the town had long ago sprawled to the country. The setting in the pines felt like what she needed in her life now. She let the children know that she would sell the house in the spring and that her employee of the last twenty years was in the process of buying her business. Her dear companion, Jim, who had been in her life for almost ten years, had passed on the winter before. She felt such gratitude for their time together. They had enjoyed each other's company tremendously. Reflecting on Jim simultaneously brought tears to her eyes and joy to her heart. She reminisced...

And the mind slows
And the remembering flows
And the heart quickens
Life's events unwritten
Beginning with fun
All days full of sun
Every day about play
No decisions to weigh
Proceed into teens
With wisdom to glean
Relationship roads
With princes and toads
Emotions abound
Found common ground
Play became work
No duty to shirk
Going within
But where to begin?

Reviewing the life
Knowing it is ALL right
Hair turning grey
Life fades away
Passing has been won
By play — well done

February 14, 2010, saw Beth Ann's destiny complete. Her time at the Pine Forest Senior Residence had given her many moments to explore the gifts in her life. She could view it with clarity and, for the most part, gratitude. The sewing and quilting she and some of the other residents did was very satisfying. They created many blankets and quilts with love and donated them to where they were needed. The chatty conversations became therapy for all. Beth Ann felt her restlessness abate more as time went on. The vacancy she felt in her soul was filled, and contentment settled in. Through all of her years, she came to understand we truly are here for only a visit so let us simply enjoy the ride. She could hear George calling to her now, "Good morning, pretty lady. Join me for coffee," and so she did.

Dream Home

The sleeplessness was really getting to Isabella. *What's going on?* she wondered. The home she had moved into last month was the closest to a dream home she had ever imagined. She was walking distance to the water, her job, shopping, and restaurants. That she even ended up in the neighbourhood was such an amazing turn of events.

Isabella was considering a job offer in another city when her good friend Lily told her about the cozy house with great location that had come up for rent while the owners were going on a sabbatical to India for two years. Upon seeing the house, Isabella was inspired to change her home situation instead of her job location. She immediately felt comfortable in the house so the fact that she was having trouble sleeping and was now also waking up recalling unusual and sometimes heart-pounding dreams was puzzling to her. Some of her friends would talk about not being able to sleep around the full moon or if they ate certain foods, but Isabella never had that problem. She could sleep easily and woke up without an alarm, feeling rested. The dreams were troubling. She just couldn't make heads or tails out of them. Isabella decided she needed to search out information with the hope that she would be able to connect the dots in her dreams. She found a lot of information in books and on the Internet.

Isabella pondered the relevance of sitting in a wooden chair, starring at an abacus in front of her. The emotion she felt as she recalled the dream was uncomfortable because it brought troubling thoughts about her relationship with her father to the forefront. She recalled the huge resistance she felt to her father. She thought about how much she wanted to count on him but never could. He was quite simply not available emotionally or physically because his job took him away often. She realized that by her father's very actions, she had learned to count on herself and had become a very confident self-sufficient person. Isabella realized that she needed to reconfigure or recalibrate old thoughts about her father into new ones of gratitude for truly she had a satisfying life. She felt lighter somehow after releasing the old thoughts and no longer had the abacus dream.

In another dream, Isabella found herself in some type of war zone. Shrapnel was flying everywhere, and she felt herself being hit by some of it. She didn't recognize the source of it, but as she reflected on the dream in the morning, she remembered events at one of her first big jobs as a lawyer. She was given a case that was supposed to be pretty straightforward. It was to be a no-fault divorce with shared custody of two teenaged children. The couple had a prenuptial agreement, so the financial aspects of the divorce were clear. What wasn't clear, however, were why the grandparents on both sides wanted to have a legal say in the children's future. All of the sudden, Isabella found herself hearing from not only the couple but also both sets of their parents with polar opposite views on religion and general upbringing of the two children. She truly felt like she was getting it from all sides. And because it was her first significant case, she wanted to be able to handle it competently on her own. That was not to be. More lawyers were involved, and at a significant cost to all parties, a settlement was eventually reached satisfactorily kind of for all involved. The children's needs finally took priority. Isabella realized that the residue of that experience had remained with her, and now she needed to finally glean the wisdom from it and release the rest. Egos had run amuck in that situation for many involved, including her for not wanting to ask for additional help. Knowing that now fully helped her to recognize the wisdom offered to her from that challenge. That unsettling dream left her, too.

The ticking in another dream kept Isabella awake by the hour. It seemed so loud and relentless. *Tick, tock, tick, tock, round and round goes the grandfather clock.* What was that about? Her office had had bomb threats in the past, but nothing serious and not in the past year. Was she running out of time? Was it time for something else? The thought began to settle into her awareness that indeed she had been allowing herself to consider her own biological clock ticking. Could that be it? She acknowledged where she was with that idea. True, she considered having her own children. Somehow, though, in her heart, she could feel that children weren't going to be part of this earth journey. She had become very committed instead to working on projects involving children in war zones. The realization came to her that perhaps she needed to affirm that she was very much at peace with the decision to not have her own biological children. And that, yes, time was running out for that, but time was ticking on for many more endeavours. The tick tock dreams stopped.

The horoscope dream was kind of spooky for Isabella. In the dream, she was in a dark room sitting at a table. The woman across from her with the creepy smile and creepier nails was telling her all about being born under her astrological sign and what she could expect because of that. The feeling in the dream was very uncomfortable, and Isabella was experiencing fear from what she was being told. When she awoke, she had an instant sense of the why of that dream.

Isabella loved searching out her horoscope and doing her own readings with a card app on her iPhone. She noticed that she was using these tools more and more and was not trusting her inherent knowing as much. She also knew this wasn't good because she really did have good instincts, and when she trusted them, they were always bang on. She was becoming lazy by using the horoscope and card apps. The message was clear to her: *Trust your own instincts and do not be led by what others say. Use the cards and horoscope as confirmation or reference or fun, but not as a go-to.* The creepy lady dreams ceased.

And what was with the being chased by a bear dream? Isabella wondered. She would awaken from that one feeling panicked and breathless. Her grade school principal came to mind as she reflected on this dream. He could certainly be described as dominating, overbearing, and intimidating. It seemed like such a long time ago to Isabella and seemed so inconsequential until she allowed herself to truly feel into what that experience was like for her. Her preteen self felt afraid. She now recalled more of her classmates feeling fearful as well. And one particular classmate was chastised by this principal with a yardstick. Isabella's twelve-year-old self felt such agony for her classmate. She felt compassion and empathy for him, and as she thought of him now, she sent loving kind energy to him. Those dreams abated as well.

That percolating coffeepot dream was a puzzler for Isabella. She recalled it vividly because it probably happened ten or twelve times before she decided to address it. So in the dream no matter where she went — the market, jogging, her job, her friend's house — there was the sound of a percolating cof-feepot. It was so very annoying, and even when she arrived at home, a coffeepot was percolating on the stove in the dream. Well, "wake up and smell the coffee" came to mind to Isabella when discerning the dream. Also the thought came to her about an idea that had been percolating in her mind about connecting with a colleague on her pro bono work with disadvantaged children. She connected with her colleague and shared the idea that had been on her mind daily. It turned out to be one of the most satisfying endeavours she had ever undertaken. She felt so much gratitude for acknowledging the dream and pursuing its relevance in her life.

Isabella's dream home had totally become her dream home. The more she was able to acknowledge what was happening, the better she was able to sleep and the sooner she was able to connect the dots in the dreams. It became a new kind of education while she was kind of sleeping...

Oh, what a dream
Awake with a scream
Goblins and ghosts
Or just odd tree-shaped posts
Shivers up the back of the spine
Droplets of blood or spilled red wine
Spirits pass by with barely a swish
Anxiety mounts — calm is the wish
Squeaking floorboards
Creepy crawlies in hoards

HOME

Wind in the trees
Weak in the knees
Chased by a bear
Escape by a hair
Shortness of breath
Like living death
Daybreak arrives
Did I survive?
Imagination is tamed
Logic regained
Face to the sun
New day begun
Nightmares erased
Light now embraced

And what about tossing and turning last night?
Isabella thought. She pondered what she had done
late into the evening and concluded that it was most
likely related to overindulging in her favourite wine,
cheese, crackers, olives, and pickles. She smiled and
felt a great love for this fun dream home.

Leaving Home

"Holy smokers! Why are you using that rickety old ladder to paint way up there, Lucinda?" asked Craig.

Craig could see his girlfriend struggling with a paint can on an extension ladder outside their older home as she tried to reach the very tip of a gable end. It truly was Lucinda's way to push limits and boundaries. Her direct conversation and abrupt manner had created more than a few predicaments in the past and quite possibly always would. Craig had been attracted to her determination and courage but found it was always best for him to remain neutral in whatever the latest Lucinda "adventure" might be.

There was the time old Mr. Lester down the road was determined to spray all the dandelions in the neighbourhood, despite Lucinda's desire to cultivate an organic yard. Craig felt it was best to simply bow out of the conversation. Sparks flew initially, but eventually a solution was reached. Mr. Lester broke his hip and needed to move to a care home. No more dandelion spray in the neighbourhood.

And then there was the time Luther Mason's dog, Pudgy, dug up all the tulip bulbs in Lucinda's flower garden. Just as Lucinda was walking over to have a loud word with Luther, Ned the neighbour's boy who was riding his bike on the sidewalk, fell right in front of her and she needed to stop to give him a hand. While she was attending to Ned, Luther's ex-wife drove up and was having a less than cordial exchange with Luther. It ended with the ex-wife loading Pudgy in her car and driving away. No more dog digging in Lucinda's flowers.

There was that unusual event when Persephonee, the palm reader two doors down, was holding a new moon drumming/chanting evening that Lucinda felt was too loud. Just when she was about to head out the door to let Persephonee know how she felt about her tunes, there was a loud thunderclap and the rain started and lasted the rest of the night. No more drumming and chanting.

Craig recalled the New Year's Eve party when Lucinda's boss had a few too many toddies and proceeded to give his loud opinion on Lucinda's tattoo. Now it wasn't a large tattoo, but it was quite conspicuous on her left hand. This situation likely wasn't going to end well, but just as Lucinda geared up with a scathing retort, her boss succumbed to his level of inebriation. No more irritating boss — for the time being, that was.

Craig didn't like to admit that maybe Lucinda was a little too easily irritated, so for the most part, he chose to quietly ignore situations. He did the bulk of the cooking in their relationship, and Lucinda did the bulk of the cleanup. He loved trying different ingredients and creating his own recipes. A favourite new dish was a veggie fritter with fresh dill sauce. It was so versatile. He could shred whatever veggies he liked picked fresh from the garden — potatoes, carrots, onions, zucchini — and fry like a pancake. The fresh dill sauce was super simple. A blend of yogurt, sour cream, chopped fresh dill, and chives. Craig found his cooking time was more of a retreat or therapy for him. And his friends loved to be on the receiving end of his delectable goodies.

There was that summer he had the pig roast. He asked everyone invited to bring their favourite mustard — homemade preferably. Twenty-three different mustards were there for a taste off with the delicious roast. Anna Taylor's was by far the favourite with her sweet and hot savoury homemade delight. Now for some illogical reason, Lucinda didn't really appreciate Anna or her mustard, and Lucinda's disposition seemed to elevate a bit in a not so positive way by the majority choosing Anna's mustard. Yes, Anna was a stunning beauty, and, yes, Anna and Craig had history together from way back in high school, and, yes, Anna did display a gentle temperament and was very kind-hearted. In Lucinda's imagination, however, Anna's homemade mustard simply wasn't the best, and so she decided she must have cheated, bought it, and put it in a mason jar.

Just when Lucinda had her accusation ready to hurl at Anna, Penny, Anna's good friend, tapped her glass to make an announcement. She began with a big thank you and applause to Craig and Lucinda for hosting such a yummy party. Next, Penny presented Lucinda and Craig with a fun antique wooden box filled with garden and greenhouse goodies. Finally, she shared that Anna and her were moving abroad to explore the castles of Europe. No more Anna and her mustard seemed to diffuse Lucinda's irritation so she was able to enjoy the party after all.

Craig was absorbed in reflecting on the many moments of uncomfortableness that were Lucinda. He was jolted out of his reverie when Lucinda offered a retort — something about how she was the only one who did any upkeep on the home so of course she was up on a ladder painting. Who else would do it?

Craig conceded in his mind that she was right. He was not getting up on a ladder to paint the gable ends. He'd prefer to maybe do some preparation and get the proper equipment, like scaffolding, but Lucinda preferred to act on impulse and did projects with little or no preparation. It was becoming more apparent to him that their differences weren't quite as "cute" as they once had been. Lucinda's ability to find fault endlessly was now tiring. It seemed his personal habits were now unacceptable to her. Craig had become accustomed to her disapproval of his choice of casual clothing, his personal grooming (or lack of), his driving skills, his mother, his friends. She did still enjoy and compliment his cooking, which was a glimmer of light in their relationship. And she seemed to experience some pleasure in their intimate exchanges. Craig focused on the positive and, indeed, relied on it to keep him plugged into their relationship...until that one day when a series of events conspired to create the perfect storm of unfavourable moments for Lucinda.

The day began with the hot water tank going on the fritz so no hot water for Lucinda's shower. She then proceeded to get dressed and found her favourite jeans wouldn't button — whether because they shrunk in the wash or she put on a pound or two was irrelevant. They no longer fit. The coffee was too strong, eggs too runny, so much going wrong, nothing was funny. Each moment seemed to bring another unacceptable event to Lucinda, and the more she focused on the unlucky day, the more irritating moments seemed to manifest.

Lucinda's boss asked her to complete a task that routinely had been her coworker's responsibility. It meant no lunch break for Lucinda. Her walk home after work was tortuously hot for a September day. She arrived home only to be met by Craig's mother, Louise, standing on the deck with pursed lips. By then Lucinda had only a fraction of her impatient patience left so, needless to say, the encounter was doomed from the start.

It seemed Craig had neglected to mention to Lucinda that his mother needed a hand with moving to a senior centre in a neighbouring town on the weekend. Louise had been waiting for them to arrive at her place, but since no one responded to her phone calls, she drove over to see what the delay was. Now Lucinda and Louise shared some similarities — one of the big ones was that they both demanded more than they asked, and both had expectations of the same man that were a little over the top. So when Craig's mother's tone was such that Lucinda felt her last nerve break, just as Craig came around the house from the backyard, both women shot words at him that would have had most others cowering. Craig, however, had become accustomed to that tone and the venom that went with it. He heard both ladies out, but then Lucinda added a new twist. Included in her attack now was that his latest creation in the kitchen, his crazy new cake, the one he had so enjoyed creating, wasn't good enough. Craig walked away.

"Greetings from the island,"
Answered the voice on the phone.
"I am at the highlands,
Needing a new zone."
"Well, take the ferry over,"
Laughed the welcoming friend.
"We can pour back some rovers,
The island's home-brewed blend."
"Sounds like perfect timing.

Partner turfed me out.
Face no longer smiling.
Cohabitation in doubt.
My habits are displeasing
To her it now seems.
No amount of appeasing,
Just greeted with screams.
Seems it's offensive — scratching and sniffing
And pulling and tugging
Also splashing and swishing
Oh, and picking and bugging.
I wish that was it,
But this list isn't complete
Cause there's also a fit
About some stinky feet.
Now, friend, I can take
A lot of ill will,
But saying my cake
Is akin to bar swill?
That's it — no more playing
This tit a tat game.
What I am saying
Is goodbye old flame."

Three years had passed since that last-straw day, and Craig found he could reflect on it now without feeling any resistance about his years with Lucinda. He did get his mother moved that weekend and gathered a few of his personal belongings from his home. He didn't even care enough to gather up his kitchen gadgets. He simply wanted to be gone, so he left. Off to the island...

As far as Craig was concerned, not having any interaction with his ex-girlfriend was worth walking. And Lucinda, for her part, must have felt a smidge of kindness as she shipped his kitchen gadgets to him. Craig's passion for his new business venture — a food truck aptly named Craig Cooks — brought a lot of joy and enthusiasm and revenue to his life. He was beginning to understand that indeed he needed to feel gratitude to Lucinda for being so difficult. Her crankiness ultimately snapped him out of his apathy and motivated him to create change and become engaged in his life. And as for Lucinda, well, she found a new passion. An encounter with a homeless kitten in the backyard opened her heart, and she started volunteering at the local animal shelter and ended up changing professions and now works full time with animals. All of their twists and turns and ups and downs assisted them both in arriving home.

Haniel's Home

Haniel awoke with a sensation of being between worlds. *Is it possible that was a dream? It felt beyond real...hhmm...could my physical body exist in the way I saw/felt?* She paused in an attempt to recapture the essence of where she just was, but somehow, it now eluded her.

Haniel proceeded to prepare for her day... Tuesday...a day for spending time with the seniors, or wisdom keepers, as she often felt they were. She loved the pace of life of the seniors. They were so present to this moment yet imparted the wisdom of days gone by so vividly. She particularly enjoyed "old Jeb," as he was known at the centre — Jebediah Sparks. And he truly sent out sparks throughout his days — some with laughter, others not so much.

Jeb walked with a stick he had carved many years before from saguaro cactus wood. It was well worn and carried the essence of the man in its rugged carvings. Haniel could generally find him in the garden area of the centre, receiving from the plants and communing with the birds, invariably in his flannel shirt, khaki trousers, and three-quarter-length worn leather coat. The spark in his blue eyes seemed so much brighter in the garden.

Haniel found him there on this Tuesday. She greeted him with her customary smile, and he responded with a nod. "How goes the morning, Jeb?" Haniel asked.

"Perfunctory," he replied.

Okay, she thought. "What does that mean, Jeb?" she asked.

"Routine," he replied. "The ability to be present here in this garden, this life, and feel no resistance to life's twists and turns yet still receive from life and be present to this gift."

"Holy smokers! All right thanks for that, Jeb." *I wish that was what routine meant to me,* she thought. "How did you arrive at that space of thought?" she asked.

"I arrived through the culmination of many lifetimes and moments of being."

Haniel was in her thirties as compared with Jebediah's octogenarian age, yet she felt comfortable and could easy feel the wisdom of what he was saying — an inner knowing of a shared communication many lifetimes ago.

Feeling comfortable in their shared silence, Haniel suddenly felt transported to another time and place. The scene unfolding before her included a camel, heat, desolation, and in the distance maybe a village. She also felt Jeb beside her as inextricably they became absorbed into the scene. There was no sense of anxiety or fear, only a willingness to be present to what this experience could bring. She felt a tingling to her skin as she shielded her eyes from the midday sun and an eagerness to proceed with this moment. *Where/what is this existence?* Haniel's analytical mind engaged briefly and then subsided as she began to further absorb her surroundings. The visual unfolding became a rhythm within her. She had an understanding, a knowing, a comprehension of this time that defied logic, and then an awareness of the wisdom of that experience became fully conscious to her. A remembering took place. She looked into Jebediah's eyes with recognition of another life, and with gratitude and appreciation she thanked him. He had tears in his eyes as he, too, became aware of the wisdom of that life. He looked upon Haniel and saw the love in her eyes and knew they had come from a life of much pain to an awareness of acceptance and understanding. All truly was well.

The more Haniel acknowledged the awareness within her, the more events continued to come to the surface. She had more encounters, more remembering, more wisdom gleaned from many lifetimes or maybe parallel lifetimes. This heralded a new time in her life, and she embraced it fully. Often, situations that once troubled her now simply faded to black.

She was recalling a perfect day. The day started with beautiful sunshine illuminating the waves rolling in on the Pacific Ocean. Haniel and her friend Liam were on a drive along the coast. There was a sense of fun and receiving from the sea. Lunch was the best halibut, chips, coleslaw, and iced tea they had ever tasted. The mood was light and open from morning until evening, and at the end of the day, a feeling of gratitude permeated every cell of her being. *Is this truly how simple life can be?* she wondered. *No schedule, no agenda, no drama —just an inner knowing of being aware and present to every breath...with joy and fun, allowing our own spark of light to shine. Goodness...okay...how does this translate into my everyday existence?* she pondered.

The awareness that people have the ability to materialize into other existences through frequency was becoming a part of Haniel's life. It went beyond a remembering. A familiarity to it captured the very essence of her being. She began to get comfortable with popping into other frequencies. For Haniel, it became simply as real and tangible as her "Earth" being.

One day, as Haniel was walking in her neighbourhood, she was drawn to a tree. She had passed this tree many times before, but now she felt the need to stop. The tree was a large oak, and she placed her palms on the tree. A peacefulness and lightness crept through her body. She felt renewed and filled. Thoughts of Jebediah receiving in the garden popped into her mind. *This is how he must feel when he is in his garden,* she thought. It felt like the satisfaction of drinking water when you are very thirsty. The feeling of being filled or renewed was just so perfect and humbling.

Another day, while Haniel was walking the beach with her sister Ellie, they had a super fun extraordinary happening. They were reminiscing about a good friend from days gone by who had passed on. They were laughing and enjoying the remembering when, suddenly, Ellie felt something wet on the top of her head. She exclaimed, "Did a bird just crap on my head?!" But neither of them had noticed a bird fly by.

Haniel looked at the top of Ellie's head. Sure enough, there was a fresh white plop on her head. They laughed as Haniel wiped the spot off Ellie's head and credited the sense of humour of their friend on the other side with popping in on their frequency to play a practical joke. *Goodness, another example of the interconnectedness of all worlds,* Haniel thought.

There was a sun-cloud mix in the sky on this early spring day as Haniel set out for her invigorating walk to the senior centre. The morning felt uncomfortable from the moment Haniel opened her eyes. She felt that something new was coming. She was looking so forward to this day as she had missed her visit the week before.

Sally, the matron of the centre, was in the reception area when Haniel entered. She caught Haniel's eye and motioned for her to join her in her office. From Sally's expression, Haniel knew something sad was coming. Jeb had passed on peacefully in his sleep during the night. Haniel caught her breath. Jeb had been one of those people who inspired her so much in the time she had been coming to the centre, and she felt such extraordinary gratitude for the blessing of knowing him. Sally had more news for Haniel. She said that Jeb had left specific instructions in writing for his belongings. He wanted her to receive the saguaro stick he had hand-carved many years before. Haniel felt very moved by this kind gesture as she knew how much the stick meant to Jeb. Haniel received it in gratitude, and on her walk back home that day, she walked with the stick and reflected on the man Jebediah Sparks, who had walked this earth with this very stick for much of his life. She realized that she felt his presence more now than when he was physically there, and it was comforting to her.

When Haniel arrived home, she placed the stick by her end table that had special shells and rocks she had collected during her many beach walks. She made a cup of tea and sat down in her comfy chair to reflect on the day's events. She picked up Jeb's stick and held it once again, closing her eyes. The image of Jeb came to her quickly and appeared to be a younger version of him and just as full of spark as when he walked the earth. His knowing smile conveyed to Haniel that his wisdom was available to her always. Tears streamed out of her eyes as she felt the love and gratitude from him. *Thank you Jeb. Thank you.* She traced the carvings on the stick with her fingers and became immersed in the tree it once was — the mighty saguaro, the tree of the desert, standing tall like a sentinel watching over the vastness of the rugged terrain. She felt the gift of this tree, its nourishing desert fruit, and once again felt the interconnectedness of all that is.

Awakened with a sense of uncomfortableness, Haniel paused before getting out of bed. She began to inhale and exhale thoughts for a peace-filled day. When the uncomfortable feelings surfaced again throughout her busy Wednesday, she would pause and breathe and reaffirm in her mind positive thoughts. It became one of those days having synchronicity or rhythm or flow or fun.

Haniel's final task before the walk home was to check in at her favourite juice bar and coffee shop, Juva's, to see whether they still needed her to help out on Saturday. Haniel filled in there occasionally on the weekends. She loved the exchange of conversation and energy with the staff and customers, learning how to make delicious fresh juices and delectable baked goods, like her favourite cinnamon twists, and the smells of fresh ground coffee and brewed teas. It never seemed like work to her. It was busy when she arrived so she paused on a stool and took in the space.

Haniel's eyes were drawn to a young man with a service dog at a corner table. He seemed familiar to her somehow. She decided to approach him and introduce herself. "Hello, my name is Haniel. How are you?"

The young man smiled and said his name was Seth and his service dog's name was Luke. Then he said, "Are you the Haniel I went to school with back in Salem?"

She smiled, "Seth Shoman, is that you? I knew there was something familiar about you. Well, school was a long time ago—

"Fifteen years, I believe," Seth said. "Some days it feels like yesterday, and some days it feels like another lifetime. Please, sit down."

She obliged, and they engaged in a conversation that lasted until closing time. To Haniel, it felt like time had simply blinked. Seth recounted many experiences that could have brought him to an unhappy outcome, but somehow, through it all, he gleaned the wisdom from it. Although his physical sight was gone, he had acquired a brand new vision for life. And in the process, he had discovered additional "senses" he didn't know he had or even existed.

Haniel confirmed her Saturday shift at Juva's, and then she and Seth left together for the walk home. They discovered through the course of their conversation that they lived on the same block. Seth had recently moved there so was just getting familiar with the area. The connection they were both feeling to one another was so familiar that it was almost unnerving, yet, in school, they were not drawn to one another in this way. Well, tomorrow was another day, so they decided to continue with their catch-up then. *What a surprisingly wonderful perfect encounter,* Haniel thought.

The day dawned sunny, and although Haniel offered to go to Seth's to pick him up, he explained that Luke was his eyes now, and he could walk to her place for a morning coffee. Seth also shared with her about his new awareness with his third eye where he's almost able to physically view his surroundings. He arrived just as the dew was disappearing from the strength of the sun.

Seth was drawn to an area of Haniel's home immediately. She walked him through the setup of the room he was in and showed Seth to her comfy chair. His hand was drawn towards the corner where Jeb's walking stick was. Haniel picked up the stick and placed it in Seth's hand, explaining to him that it was from a very special friend of hers. He asked her to give him a moment as he began to receive from the saguaro stick. A smile formed on his face and grew brighter as he embraced the knowledge and wisdom carried within the humble walking aid.

"This man," Seth said, "I know the man who carried this stick, Haniel. I know him now like I knew him then. We were once warriors together. We watched out for one another always. I felt our ship going down, and together we were able to jump into the sea and get on a small life boat and paddle to shore. It feels like the area of the Mediterranean Sea. We both loved you, Haniel. I can feel the ache, the longing we had to return home, but it was not to be. We were able to help a woman and her children to safety before forging on towards home. The miles stretched long before us. My friend's foot was sore, so I managed to carve him a walking stick out of one of the few larger olive trees. The stick was quite gnarled but served the purpose. Our bodies continued to weaken as there was not much fresh water. We eventually succumbed to a plague that ravaged our weakened bodies quickly. We were within five miles of home."

When Seth finished his story, Haniel continued to sit in silence. She had been feeling the recounting of the events and found herself in a state of remembering. She felt the longing of that time — always stopping to look down the road to see if anyone was coming — the passage of time as the months turned to years and no one returned to her. She worked in an infirmary, and, though, at times was weak, she was able to stay alive by sheer will. Haniel could feel the essence of that determination with her today. The ability to harness the will, the determination, to forge ahead and thrive was what sustained her then — and now, she realized. It was comforting somehow.

And then Haniel had a thunderbolt of awareness. While recalling her previous life, she realized parts of her heart had simply closed off — shut down during that time — and stayed that way. In her life today, she remained cautious in matters of the heart, not fully recognizing why until now. Tears flowed now as she acknowledged with gratitude this awareness and felt the path of heart healing available to her now. Without hesitation, she seized the opportunity and opened her heart.

Seth continued to feel the awareness of Jebediah. They had been like brothers, true friends. This "viewing" he was experiencing with his third eye was so tangible and real. He could feel the climate, smell the season, and experience the sensation of putting one foot in front of the other on the hard-packed earth. The topography was unforgiving yet hauntingly beautiful.

Haniel and Seth reached for each other's hands simultaneously and were transported to an extraordinary awareness of time and space. The limitlessness of the journey was breathtaking. The recognition and connection of their friend Jebediah was brought fully to them now. This was not thought; they were feeling into the essence of their friend. There was a sense of "home" that went beyond any earthly words. This knowledge teleported Seth and Haniel to an awareness that was breathtaking. Could they remember more Earth lives, and would it be relevant and helpful to embark on this train of thought? These words came to Haniel's mind...

A whispered hope, a helping hand
A heartfelt cry, an embracing land
Reaching afar for visions unseen
Finding truth within what once has been
Perils and hardships revealing all
Soul's truth saying, "It was worth the fall"

Walking, running, rising to more of life
So much wisdom from those days of strife
And now a new day dawning for us
Not really necessary to stew and fuss
Sparks of light surrounding us now
We laugh, we love, we take a bow
Well done, earth soul, with your game
Grateful to acknowledge, there's no one to blame
Gliding ahead, like flocks of geese
Helping one another to always know peace

Haniel felt her whole being exhale through the expression of these words. The wisdom of lifetimes was now inherent within her, and she felt it to her very core — another opportunity for a heart opening moment in her life. She held Seth's hand and felt an expansion from her heart. *Could we elevate our lives with this heart light? Truly, we can,* they both felt the answer instantly. Throughout the morning, Seth's dog, Luke, had been quietly laying at Seth's feet. Quite suddenly, Luke made an unusual noise, almost sounding like "Yahoo!" as if to say, "You humans are tapping into something perfect." Haniel was both startled and amazed as she realized fully the divine assistance offered by Luke. All creatures great and small came to mind to Seth.

"We are all connected, all one. Pretty simple, Haniel," Seth said. "Our connections transcend all time, space, and dimension."

Oh, the possibilities. For the first time in this life, Haniel felt home.

Happier Home

She and Jeremy were destined to be together. She felt it for sure. How could they not? Jolene was eighteen when she first saw thirty-two-year old Jeremy. Still, she was sure that he was the guy was for her. So she was still in high school, no problem. *We will figure life out day by day,* she thought. Her parents' disapproval to the relationship didn't impact her decision to continue to see Jeremy.

Jolene felt that spending time with him was an escape and relief from her regular life. The rest of her life paled in comparison, so she let her studies go as well as many other obligations. With all of the squabbling her parents did, she really didn't feel they could offer sage advice, or any advice for that matter. And besides, she and Jeremy really did have a passion for one another.

Jeremy was a hardworking man, very driven in his business, and often spent long hours accomplishing the many tasks of running his thriving water company. Jolene started working with him, doing clerical tasks to begin with. She was a quick learner, so it wasn't long before she was able to do any task — from dealing with suppliers to overseeing the bottling, to driving the delivery trucks. Her versatility and eagerness to learn proved her to be indispensable in a very short time. Jolene was also quite savvy with social media, which enhanced the business further.

As their business grew, so did their family. Within ten years, Jolene and Jeremy married, had two children, and expanded the business to neighbouring communities. They had a staff of about thirty people and, for the most part, were pleased with the people they hired. Jolene felt grateful for all that had transpired in her life, but somehow, she simply could not make peace with her parents. Their relationship had remained cordial over the years, and with the birth of her children, her parents seemed more loving but still reserved or distant. For Jolene, becoming a parent was such a heart-opening experience that it brought the awareness of how uncomfortable her parents were to the forefront. She used to simply feel that was just who they were, but now she felt compelled to have a conversation with them, and she decided to start with her dad.

Jolene went to visit her father on a Friday morning when she knew her mother would be out golfing with her friends. She found him in the backyard weeding the small garden.

"Good morning, Father," she said.

He returned the greeting and continued with his project. They discussed a few topics before Jolene could settle enough to ask him some heart-to-heart questions. She began with explaining to her father that she was uncomfortable with needing to have this conversation with him but felt it was necessary. She asked why her parents were so distant with her and each other and why for as long as she could remember they did not share a loving relationship. Her father silent for a while, which made Jolene think her questions would not be answered. Finally, her father looked at her and suggested they go and sit on the chairs nestled between the climbing roses.

He took his time, and as he looked off into the distance, tears formed in his eyes. "Your mother and I met when we were teenagers. I was very attracted to her outgoing personality, and we were comfortable with each other and became good friends. There was much to admire about her, and other guys were interested in her as well. We lived this rural life, and there was an assumption that young folks married, had children, and remained in the same town until old age. We were no exception to this way of life. Our summer jobs became our careers — your mom at the grocery store, eventually managing it, and me at the garage. We were ill prepared to become parents or a couple, but we forged ahead thinking this is what we should do. Both of us were overjoyed at your birth Jolene, and we have had no regrets about becoming parents, but...I'm at a loss as to how to express what happened next," he said to his daughter.

Jolene suddenly felt that maybe she never should have come to her father with her questions. He now had a tortured expression on his face, and the tears began to flow.

"I have not shared this part of myself for many years, Jolene, and I'm finding it difficult to voice my words," he finally said.

Jolene's father proceeded to bare his soul to his daughter. Over the course of the next hour, her father revealed his heart to her in a way she never imagined. Her parents had agreed to remain married and raise Jolene together, even though her dad came to the realization that he was a gay man. This was something not really understood or spoken about in their rural community or with their generation.

How heartbreaking this must be for both of them, Jolene thought. She hoped that by her father unburdening himself, perhaps her parents could go forth in truth, honesty, and possibly release each other from their contract. Jolene's mother returned home about this time, so the opportunity to continue the conversation as a family presented. Her mother showed a lot of resistance initially, but when she realized her daughter wished to help them and was not judging them, her icy core began to melt.

A lot of tears flowed that afternoon. A dialogue was opened, and a whole new world seemed available to Jolene's parents. Both had buried their feelings over the years, and now they were allowed to surface. Jolene began to view them not only as her mom and dad but as Doreen and Sam — young teenagers, eagerly anticipating life. She wondered and so asked her parents why, once she had left home, they didn't proceed with their lives independent of one another. They looked at each other and struggled with a response. It seemed they were both afraid, now in their fifties, to start new lives without each other. In many ways, they were friends and depended on one another heavily and weren't sure how to proceed without each other.

The decision was based on fear, and now Jolene felt it could be helpful if they both faced their fears. She let them know she loved them and was grateful to them and also that she supported them with whatever decisions they arrived at within their lives. There was no place for secrets with life anymore. What revelations could be ahead for them if they both chose to lead authentic lives?

As Jolene drove home, feelings of relief flooded through her. It was the first time she felt like a family with her parents. She also decided to give her parents some time before sharing their circumstances with Jeremy and the children.

Over the next five years, many changes happened within the family dynamic. Her parents became more comfortable with their situation and shared it openly with Jolene and her family. They separated, remaining close, and both moved to a larger city nearby. It became a lesson in love, understanding, compassion, and humanity for Jolene. Her parents were closer after their separation than they ever were married.

The wisdom from that relationship came fully into Jolene's awareness with her husband's words one day. It seemed he was questioning their relationship, and, truly, so was Jolene. They were having an increasingly difficult time finding common ground within their marriage. They had their children and the business, but that's where it ended, and they both knew it needed to be addressed. Neither of them wanted to upset the apple cart, so Jeremy began the conversation. He was an introverted soul by nature and was now finding he wanted more solitude in his life. Jolene recognized their differences had become large and harder to ignore but had always felt it was okay. Their children were about to leave home, and even though both were involved working with the business, Jolene and Jeremy had encouraged them to take time for postsecondary education. It meant they would be spending time in the city and home some weekends and holidays. Jeremy and Jolene's lives were so intertwined it seemed such a huge challenge for any kind of separation to work out amicably. Reflection brought much to the surface for Jolene....

I was thinking one day, about times gone by

Track meets, record hops, days of junior high

And I was thinking about sharing conversations with friends

Meeting at the river, wishing the day would never end
And I was thinking about the time when I met you
How it changed my world and I began something new
Knowing love and loving in a sweet new way
Awakening to each moment, embracing every day
Hearts now expanded, Mommy and Daddy our new names

So much fun, playing this earth game
Time passed, and we travelled on
Tasks, words, tears — we formed a bond
With not much fanfare or warning it seemed
Looking at one another with emotions unforeseen
Life and marriage became undefinable terms
Rotating in our minds like a fever or germ
Suddenly the ring became a chain of gold
Wanted for its richness but not for its hold
Could our hearts expand beyond this emotion?
Could we once again feel that level of devotion?
We paused, and we cried,
And we loved, and we lied
Sad and lonely as I see him walking away
Wisdom gleaned and carried to another day

Jolene was able to release the death-grip attachment she had to Jeremy and the marriage eventually. And she was able to release him unconditionally — eventually. And inexplicably their lives resumed with Jolene knowing for sure that because of her parents' relationship, she was able to greet her next chapter with a measure of eagerness and wisdom. The meaning of home was redefined, and a happier home was created. Through waves of sadness and loneliness, authenticity emerged.

Heritage Home

Dave attached the lockbox back onto the gate after completing the Sunday afternoon open house. It was a fairly successful showing. The weather had cooperated so, in total, twenty-three people had come through the door. For Dave, that was positive because the listing was in a difficult location. It took two ferries from the mainland to get to the island that the dwelling was on, so it was not a fit for a lot of potential buyers. The owner had built there for seclusion but now found that he wasn't able to get to the island nest often because his job location had changed. The waterfront cabin was rustic but did have electricity, an outdoor sauna, a hot tub, and a great fresh water collection system. Fishing was available right off the aluminum dock as well as swimming, water sports, and boating.

The significant interest had net two offers from the open house. Dave was looking forward to a close on this listing as he had a few other deals pending that required more of his attention. The real estate company he worked with encompassed a variety of listings, so for Dave, it kept the job interesting. There were housing opportunities available at every price point and size. The ability to be able to connect with people from all walks of life was something Dave had cultivated from a young age. He was raised in a housing development in the busy inner city. It was multicultural so opened his eyes to different walks of life, ultimately preparing him well for this profession.

Dave had recently been selling micro-apartments in the thriving downtown core. The average size of these dwellings was 300 square feet, and they were so well designed that there had been a great response, and the building had sold out quickly. Demand had exceeded supply. It intrigued Dave immensely that 300 square feet was perfect for some people, and 4,000 square feet was too small for others. *Good thing humans are diverse,* he mused. *Great for business.*

His next open house was at a development by a small lake for people fifty-five and older. This was a growing demographic that Dave was happy to address as financing usually didn't come into play. The development he was showing was gated duplex homes with attached garages and shared amenities. Although the average size was smaller than previous fifty-five-plus developments — originally at 1,200 square feet and these at 900 — he was confident that this size would be appealing. These homes had an attractive price for the location, so the developer was optimistic that they would sell quickly. And they did. Indeed, there was a market for creating these mini villages. They were also in the preliminary development of creating a tiny home community. It was diversification for the company, but with the popularity of tiny homes increasing, they wanted to be a part of this interesting twist in housing.

These homes were self-contained and portable, creating some parallels with travel trailers or RVs but with more of a home feel and design. Dave was enthusiastic for this project to come to fruition as it also addressed green living, something very much in the consciousness of the millennial demographic. There was also the potential for tiny homes to be placed in the backyards of some city homes where zoning allowed for this temporary housing feature — perhaps a "granny flat" option. Dave found many people their forever homes, but for him personally, renting a condo remained his comfort zone. To him, home meant a place to shower in the morning and sleep in at night. He wasn't particular about decor or trends for himself, even though it was so relevant in his job. His life was consumed with work — something he enjoyed a lot and didn't leave time for much of anything else.

Dave didn't often feel like connecting on a more personal level with his clients, but for some reason, he was unusually drawn to the woman sitting across from him at his desk this Monday morning. He had her pegged at fortyish but wasn't confident of that number either. Her name was Phoebe, and she was interested in finding out the value of her family home and possibly listing it. Dave offered to check out the home with her and determine what was best from there. The heritage home had been in her family for many generations, so it offered a great lot size from the original time period.

Dave could see upon driving up to the home that, externally, it was in need of some repair. When they went inside, although it was historically beautiful, the need for updating showed. The dramatic spiral staircase with its ornate spindles captured Dave's attention. So much craftsmanship was evident in the creation of this home. Phoebe revealed that as a young boy her great-grandfather had helped his father with the building of the home. She knew the history intimately and could tell a story for every part of the home. Her ancestors had arrived in this part of the world over 150 years ago after leaving a life of some affluence in Europe. They settled and built a thriving import business. As far as descendants, each generation had only one child so Phoebe now found herself to be the sole heir of this extraordinary home. She was very torn in regards to the next step for this generational home. It was up to her either to carry on the legacy of this home or to sell it and trust that a new owner would do what was best for the heritage beauty.

When Dave completed his tour of the house, he confirmed to Phoebe what she already knew. It would cost probably a minimum of $300,000 to restore the interior and $200,000 for the exterior and yard. It wasn't an outrageous amount, but it was significant. This was more than Phoebe was willing to or could comfortably commit to this home. Dave let her know if she sold the dwelling with restorations complete, she could ask well over $1 million, but if she sold it as it was, she could ask about $500,000.

Phoebe understood the numbers, but it was the emotion that was difficult to make peace with. Her ancestors came to the country and physically, with their own hands, built this home. She could not come up with a definitive answer in regards to her obligation to her family's history. She recalled summers spent at the home with her parents and grandparents. Yes, it had been idyllic but also lonely. Her father was an only child, and now she was an only child. And she did not have children of her own and was uncertain she would, not to mention burdening any future child with the responsibility of the home. Her travels had taken her all over the world. She had traced her family history in Europe and came to appreciate the courage they had in embarking on a new life in a new country. And through all of her years of backpacking through many countries, she came to know the many versions of home.

Colourful row houses in a fishing village
Wrought-iron gates by ocean villas
Condos with views of downtown or mountains
Gated communities with entrance fountains
Float homes, park models, casitas, or RVs
Choices and options so many to glean

Living abroad at a beach or rainforest
Finding a spot where breezes are warmest
Maybe a flat above a pub, in an old English town
Perhaps a remote cabin, a place to slowdown
Bungalow, bilevel, split level, and rancher
What's the solution and best possible answer?
Mature neighbourhoods with heritage homes
And yards with gardens and room to roam
Farm houses and ranches offering a
rugged sentiment
And nostalgia for days when pioneering
was prevalent
Towering apartments offering convenience
and location
Carrying the scents and sounds of many a nation
So many offerings and options to ponder
Could home be truly in the wild blue yonder?

Dave decided to do some additional research to assist Phoebe with her dilemma. He discovered the possibility of a restoration grant for heritage homes in that part of the city. He met with Phoebe to discuss this option. She would be required to submit a full history on the dwelling and donate the land and building to the heritage foundation. If it fit the criteria, the foundation would then maintain the home. It was an intriguing idea.

Phoebe realized that Dave would lose potential commission with this option, so she asked him about that. Her directness caught him off guard initially, but he felt comfortable enough to share more of himself with her. Dave recognized that Phoebe had a unique attachment to the dwelling, but perhaps the knowledge of that was more of a burden than a gift. She needed to make peace with which one it was. He related his experience growing up in the inner city where family encompassed people who were blood relatives and people who were not. Neighbours depended on one another daily — whether for baby-sitting, errands, meals, or simply company. There was no going back to visit the old neighbourhood as it had been replaced with townhouses long ago.

The memories, however, remained for Dave, and for the most part, there was heartfelt nostalgia. It had been only Dave and his grandmother as his mother had passed on when he was young, and he did not know his father. Grandma did her very best for him, and he did his very best for her. He felt very fortu-nate to have her, and he stayed with her until she passed on. And now here he was telling Phoebe his story. She was the only person he ever felt inclined to share his past with. She listened intently. And then she shared her story with him. Somehow it was like they had always been friends. There were no barri-ers, and they were truly comfortable with each other. Their connection was solid and attraction mutual.

Phoebe decided to donate her heritage home to the foundation. Dave was present for support in whatever capacity was necessary. The full beauty of the extraordinary home emerged as the restora-tion progressed and Phoebe shared with Dave the memories and stories in each room. The intimacy and connectedness was elevating to both of them. Through the process of releasing the family home, Phoebe and Dave found family and home in each other.

Holistic Home

"Ouch — what the fuck?"

Jessica had to laugh with her client who was grimacing through his reflexology treatment. "My apologies, Larry," she said.

Jessica's twenty-plus years working with holistic wellness had brought some interesting exchanges with clients — they were always good and always worthwhile she found. The value and personal satisfaction of offering her services was gratifying and had opened an opportunity to expand her horizons in regards to the human condition.

Larry was one of those clients who showed up for a session every few weeks or so. He worked hard and played hard, so his body was presenting him with a few challenges. He found that reflexology alleviated some symptoms — specifically sore back and low energy — and he also noticed he slept better after a session. When doing reflexology, usually a few spots on the feet gave a bit of a bite, but the overall session always produced a level of relaxation and enjoyment. Some clients were full of banter and bubbled over with conversation, while others closed their eyes and drifted away. Jessica often felt the exchange was mutually beneficial.

Jessica enjoyed learning and sharing about what triggered a healing response in the body through applying pressure to points on the hands and feet. She recalled a client asking her whether she could push a spot on the foot to make his "member" stand up or stay down for that matter. Others requested she push the "quit smoking" spot, or the "lose weight" spot, or the "find me the perfect mate" spot, or "make me single again" spot, or the "make my wrinkles go away" spot, or "make the mother-in-law disappear" spot, and the list went on. All amusing and, for Jessica, told a story. She came to know when to share some words of wisdom, when to remain silent, when to offer a tissue or lozenge, and when to laugh. The laughter, she felt, offered the most profound healing. The endorphins released from the big belly laugh or the tears streaming down the face snorting laugh brought immeasurable results to that peaceful balanced frame of mind all strive to achieve.

For those not comfortable with the pressure of reflexology, Jessica offered Reiki and therapeutic touch work. These forms of therapy had no contraindications and offered peace to troubled minds and bodies. Clients lay on the comfortable therapy table, and Jessica performed the gentle energy work by either placing her hands directly on the body or hovering them above the body. Most clients reported feeling calm and peaceful throughout the session. Holistic wellness was becoming much more common than when Jessica began her career.

Initially, Jessica was met with some resistance, but over time, people became more informed, and those searching for complimentary therapies would find her. Everything has its time, and she was feeling the time for people to take charge of their own wellness was now. Whatever she could do to ignite and achieve a healing response in people's bodies, minds, and spirits was worth exploring. And, wow, was there a lot to explore. The Internet created the opportunity to learn about any new or old or emerging therapy. How to discern the value or merit of each or any became a time-consuming challenge. What role in healing did Rolfing, Feldenkrais, Watsu, aromatherapy, chelation, biofeedback, ear candling, Bach flower remedies, homeopathy, iridology, shiatsu, astrology, kinesiology, naturopathy, live blood analysis, and Chinese medicine, to name only a few, play in creating well-being? And then there was the plethora of vitamins, herbal supplements, minerals, adaptogens, protein powders, energy bars, foods, and superfoods...and the beverages...and fermented foods...and drink red wine (but not too much)... and eat chocolate (but not too much and only dark, fair-trade organic)...and have coffee or maybe don't have coffee. Mixed messages could be found daily on what was best or not for people's well-being. *How*

*did being a healthy, balanced human become so compli-
cated?* Jessica pondered...

Seems like a lot of kale and gluten-free
And super antioxidant Japanese green tea
Measuring portions and analyzing labels
Discerning what is fact or fiction or fables
Sweet potatoes, yams, asparagus galore
Potatoes, meat, dairy — is it really no more?
Oils of oregano, lavender, and rose
Patchouli and vetiver igniting the nose
Colloidal silver considered antibiotic
Herbs with properties that are kind of narcotic
Spinning, yoga, qigong, and Thai chi
Calming the mind, helping us to just "be"
Meditations, mudras, mandalas, and mantras
Crystals, rocks, stones, sex that is tantra?
The honey, the pollen, royal jelly from the bee
The lowly dandelion, offering healing for free
From Klamath Lake, Oregon, comes E3live
Blue green algae, helping us to thrive
Coconut in anything and everything it seems
Except maybe pie — only available in dreams
Oh, yes, sorting out dreams and their meanings
Flashes, lights, images like movie screenings
Preachers and gurus talking about love
Which is right or wrong — all of the above?
Goodness the mind can really spin a yarn
Could it be all in our heads? Oh darn
If that is the case, the solution is at hand
No potion, no concoction, no trendy name brand

Simply positive thoughts and affirmations every day
Reinforcing our light and gifts along the way

Jessica recalled the meat-and-potato diet she had grown up on in the far north. They had the garden and berries in the summer, from which they preserved for the winter. They made cabbage into sauerkraut in large crocks, and they made cucumbers into pickles in quart jars. They turned moose meat into sausage and canned it in jars. The long days of summer seemed to quickly pass into the short, dark days of winter. The awareness of vitamins and nutrition was not in the consciousness as the focus was quite simply on filling the belly. Having a spoonful of molasses took care of iron deficiency, and they could chew garlic for any malady. Gargling salt water for sore throats and a bit of baking soda in water for upset stomach or urinary tract irritation were common. They made a mustard plaster for chest congestion and general aches and pains. It consisted of making a poultice out of a mustard seed powder paste and spreading it on a heavy gauze material and placing it on the body in the affected area for a limited amount of time. It was very effective in reducing pain and alleviating chest congestion. And, of course, the merits and nourishing effects of working and playing outside most of the day contributed to great natural stress relief with endorphins flooding into the system through physical exertion. It all held its relevance for then and now. Jessica had incorporated the knowledge into her approach to wellness today.

She chose her centrally located home office initially for its price, but it had proven to be a great choice for location and size. She was able to convert the street-side attached garage into an inviting office space. She replaced the garage door with large windows, which featured local stained-glass art on the central panel. Two of the windows opened, allowing for breezes to flow through to cleanse and refresh the space. The holistic room flowed from the dwelling into the yard, incorporating water features and potted herbs with flowers. All in all, it was an environment that invited a calming response.

The almost commonplace cancer diagnosis was heralding many more inquiries into what was the best bet for hurdling the disease. Checking out options on the Internet often served to create even more questions, confusion, and angst. The traditional approach seemed to achieve limited results so people were searching for more solutions. Testimonials about cannabis oil created a renewed interest in the controversial marijuana plant. Everything has its time, so perhaps the time had come for the healing potential of this plant to be harnessed and harvested. The need for the merits of all plants to be optimized was at hand with the almost epidemic diagnosis going on with many autoimmune diseases. And all of these diseases were manifesting in spite of the extraordinary wealth of information and product and awareness available.

Something was out of sync, and it became Jessica's focus to determine a simple philosophy to being human. Honouring individual choices and decisions people make as humans was the first thought to sit solidly in her mind. She asked herself, *What is the very best thing I can do upon awakening?* She immediately got the answer: *Express gratitude. Feel gratitude to the core. Do some body talk. Thank my body for carrying me around all day. Be grateful for the ability to smell the fresh earth and to drink fresh water…for being able to feel the heat of the sun, warming to the bone…for laughter and tears and joy and anger…for dirty dishes that nourishing food was on…. for sore feet asking me to rest and soak… for moodiness asking me to get outside and refresh… and, yes, for those many moments of that "what the fuck?" feeling, moments of feeling quite simply out of sync, and moments of such deep emotion surfacing bringing tears of humble gratitude for the privilege of this life. Thank you for this home.*

Finding Home

I'm in love, was Natalie's first thought as she slowly opened her eyes. The thought both surprised and pleased her. The image of Ben came to her mind. Ben with his easy smile, Ben giving so much of himself to his two sons, Ben appreciating his work, not minding shift changes and long hours.

It had been six months since Natalie had moved to the area for the nursing job. She wanted this posting initially for better pay and more hours and also to learn about working in a smaller community. It proved to be a good fit for her. The added bonus of finding love was more than the icing on the cake. Natalie had been somewhat fickle about relationships in the past. Her focus was on her career, and for the most part, she felt like she didn't have the desire for any kind of a committed relationship. There had been lonely days where the thought came to her that perhaps it was time to make more of an effort, but those days were always short lived. Thank goodness. And now, here she was at forty-two, in a committed relationship for the first time. It felt okay — well, more than okay. It felt perfect and comfortable and soul satisfying and quite simply new as she was also kind of a step-mom now. Well, the boys didn't call her "Mom"; they called her "Natalie," and she was happy with that. Their mother had passed on two years earlier, and naturally that life change was still quite raw at times.

Natalie met Ben on her first shift at the hospital. He was head nurse on the ward she was assigned to so she interacted with him a lot. She found him to be task-oriented and cordial in his approach. But on the ward, with the patients, she noticed Ben's natural kindness and empathy and sense of humour flourished. He was so natural. Patients and staff alike responded to him with so much appreciation. Natalie was working there for three months before she asked Ben if he would like to go for coffee or lunch sometime. He appeared surprised initially but agreed to meet the following day for lunch. The delicious lunch on the waterfront combined with a stimulating fun conversation led to many more lunches, and suppers, and watching the boys' soccer games, and pizza nights, and heartfelt glances, and lingering kisses. It created a desire for more within her. She had never felt that she was lacking for anything in life, but now she was discovering that the communion she felt with Ben was essential to her life. In fact, she could no longer imagine her life without him in it. The feeling challenged her as she had never felt this vulnerable before. *This must be what it feels like to be all in,* she thought, and as she welcomed it, but she also felt the hesitation...and some resistance...

Get out of your head
Remain on the ground
Great roads ahead
Experiences abound
Laughing with crying
Whispering words
Emotions flying
Hearing songbirds
Sharing the chores
Out and about
Shopping galore
Having a cookout
Traditions and holidays
New ideas to create
Some family Sundays
On the rink to skate
Kitchen smells of baking
Board games to play
Some picture taking
Rides in the sleigh
Time marching on
Little feet running
Heartfelt sweet songs
You faintly humming
Gripping the hands
Pacing the floor
Making demands
Connection restored

The stretch of night shifts was creating some irritability in Natalie. Initially, she had enjoyed the night shifts. There was something about the stillness of the night, quietly connecting with the patients, making her rounds, fetching a warm blanket or pillow, heartfelt conversations with those who sleep eluded, and the sole satisfaction of simply being present in those bewitching hours. But now, it seemed, there was always the thought popping into her mind about how Ben fit into her life. She knew she needed to totally surrender to the gift of the relationship, but the pattern of needing to control every emotion and event in her life seemed to win out. Inevitably, this created angst within her and now at her job as well. What was it in her life that drove her with the need to control? Natalie hesitated to explore the truth and wisdom of that question. She finished her shift and walked to her cozy apartment. She loved that she was only a five-minute walk from work to home. Ordinarily after a night shift, she would unwind with a cup of tea or warm bath, but on this day she went straight to bed. The question came back to her as she drifted in and out of sleep. *Why the need to control?*

Thoughts of her parents or lack of parents popped in and out of Natalie's mind as she gingerly approached the why. She allowed the memory of the venomous spats between her father and mother to emerge and allowed the emotion to surface. She realized that she was methodically organizing her thoughts and surroundings while her parents battled.

Could it be that in her child's mind she felt that if everything around her was orderly, her life would be, too, and so she carried this within her as a shield? Natalie knew the answer to that question and didn't like the feel of it. She went further down the memory trail and remembered when she was six years old and left at her grandparents' — her mother's parents — for "a few days," never to be picked up again and how she didn't know if it was okay that she was not missing her parents and that she loved her grandparents who dearly loved her.

Through the years, there had been very little communication with her parents, so Natalie had put them out of her mind. She loved school and did well, excelling in science and math. Her grandparents' home was in an old neighbourhood with lots of large trees to climb or sit under. One of her chores (though it didn't feel like a chore to Natalie) was mowing the lawn and raking those massive amounts of leaves. It smelled so invigorating and was satisfying to be out in nature. Her grandfather would often be outside with her, whistling or humming to himself with a content look on his face. Grandmother had a sadness about her but didn't share her feelings often. She busied herself with her part-time job at the library and escaped into books often. They shared the cooking and clean up daily. They had a fun routine in the kitchen. There was mashed-up Mondays, which were leftovers from usually a big Sunday dinner. Taco Tuesdays could be all veggie with a selection of beans and shredded cheese. Wednesdays, Grandpa golfed, so Natalie and her Grandma often made a favourite sandwich. Thursdays usually meant a slow cooker meal (which could be a roast or chicken or lentil soup) with enough left over for Friday. Saturday was a shopping day and sometimes dinner out or take-out.

Natalie's childhood had flow and harmony in spite of or maybe because of her parents leaving her. Her grandparents had passed on within a year of each other four years ago, and Natalie had been there for them, nursing them and loving them. She truly could not have imagined her life without them. The love Natalie and her grandparents had for one another had erased any residue from her parents abandoning her. She was able to have some conversations with her grandparents about her parents, and that was helpful. Her grandma's sadness at never being able to fully make peace with her daughter was regretful but understandable.

Natalie's grandparents had only one child, Natalie's mother, and they had indulged and spoiled her in many ways. She became hard to contain and quite rebellious in all aspects of her life. When she met Natalie's father, they impulsively took off back-packing, eventually arriving back home broke and pregnant. They married and tried to create a home environment, but both had a wild nature, constantly needing freedom and space. Natalie came to realize the wisdom her parents displayed by leaving her

— ultimately giving her a much better life. Perhaps the day would come where she would be able to reconnect with her parents — if they were still alive — but in the meantime, gratitude filled her body and soul as she drifted in and out of sleep. Finding home had not been a thought that had preoccupied her mind. Accepting, knowing, and understanding that she was home brought a new level of peace to Natalie. Home.

Sasq'ets Home

The light rain falling and misty fog obscured Leanne's view somewhat as she drove into the quaint town about ten miles off the main highway. Still, people were out and about so it took a couple of loops around town to find a parking spot for her vintage van. "Vintage" was being kind. The van really was on its last days serving her as both transportation and home.

Leanne recalled the series of events that had resulted in her purchase of the classic vehicle six years earlier. Her season of tree planting was just about to wrap up, so she was looking for her next opportunity. A coworker told her about a friend of a friend named Jon, who had a van for sale, and because Jon was moving out of the country that next week, he was open to offers. He thought he had the van sold several times, but the buyers never showed with the money. Leanne thought maybe the van was waiting for her, so she had a look at it, made an offer, and became the proud owner of the classic van. Jon was grateful to finally sell the van, so he was flexible on the price because he was in a time crunch and needed to tie up loose ends quickly.

The van suited Leanne, and she already knew what small living was about, so she didn't have to make any major adjustment to this lifestyle. At the ripe old age of thirty-two, she had a network of friends in many places, so she was able to pop in on someone she knew wherever she was and always had a spot to park the van and hang out. She even managed to be in the locale of a mechanic friend when the van required some repair. The give-and-take of this situation always panned out well because Leanne was a gifted artist, so she would create whatever the friend would like for exchange. One of the genres she excelled in was portrait artistry, which was requested often. Her van accommodated the pastels and charcoals she loved to work with. She did some busking at open air markets and festival venues, which net her a good amount of cash for her lifestyle.

When Leanne decided to make a stop at the village in the huge forest and mountains, it was mostly because she heard the stories and fables about Sasq'ets — meaning "hairy man" in the Sts'ailes First Nations language. Sasquatch and Big Foot were also handles for the fabled creature. As a ten-year veteran of tree planting, there had been moments in the forests when she was sure something was watching. Ordinarily, this didn't bother Leanne as she was educated in forest awareness with her job. However, some moments her hair really did stand up on the back of her neck and the spirit bumps on the skin took a while to abate. It was those moments of uncomfortableness that inspired Leanne to learn more about Sasq'ets, and learning more about Sasq'ets inspired her to visit the village — famed not only for the creature but also hot springs, forest hikes, and lake swimming, boating, and fishing.

Leanne arrived during a period of several days of rain, so she took this time to visit with the locals and learn as much as she could about the area. The local coffee shop hangout was a great source of current events and helpful in finding out about off-the-beaten-track camping spots. And, of course, there were the self-named local Sasquatch experts with their tales of sightings and footprints — or paw prints. The clay moulds made from the footprints and grainy photos and videos added more intrigue to the stories. It seemed there were more questions than answers. Leanne had the desire to create a drawing of the mythical Sasq'ets as she continued to explore the area.

Finally, the gloomy weather lifted, and the sun started to stream through, so Leanne set out on one of the many hiking trails that were accessible from right in the village. The trail Leanne picked was rated as difficult as it was quite steep with precarious footholds in some parts. She enjoyed the challenge and was rewarded upon reaching the summit to a view that truly was breathtaking and awe-inspiring.

Leanne paused and sat down. It was the perfect moment to rest and receive.

The sun was warm on her skin, and as she dozed lightly, images of the Sasq'ets came to her mind. She started focusing on the portrait she would create. She drifted off and felt herself viewing another world. She felt a sense of welcome as she viewed the Sasq'ets. Initially, they seemed oblivious to her, and then one turned and looked directly into her eyes. Leanne felt time stand still. The warmth and loving kindness projected to her from that gaze brought tears to her eyes. Somehow she had a complete comprehension of this extraordinary being. She also felt a sense of the purpose or reason or relevance of the Sasq'ets. The natives spoke of the Sasq'ets as originating in the spiritual realm with the ability to pop in and out of existence. This could explain why the being was considered elusive and difficult to photograph. Maybe it quite simply wasn't on the physical earth often. It seemed possible to Leanne as she connected with the spirit being. She felt a transmission of information and wisdom flowing to her and was humbled and awed by the simplicity of the message. Leanne received and connected with a frequency being, bringing the awareness to her that people communicate through frequency simply because words are not adequate to express this kind of wisdom and love. This loving kindness transcended any form of earthly wisdom. It spoke of the interconnectedness of all that is...

In the stillness of dawn
Birds break into song
Dew drops on logs
Frogs croak in bogs
Skunk cabbage odours
Dwarfed by granite boulders
Sculptures of moss
Tree limbs crisscross
Many shades of green
Appearing aquamarine
Scurrying squirrels
Above underground worlds
Images it seems
Revealed unforeseen
A face in a tree trunk
Nose protruding, eyes sunk
Ponds and trickling creeks
Marshes and waterfall streaks
Winding, fading trails
Bees buzzing, silent snails
Fog is lifting
Temperature is shifting
Sun streaking in
As the day begins
Breath creating space
Bowing with grace

Leanne emerged from her vision with a clear con-
ception of the image she would create to fully capture
the extraordinary being she had encountered. Her
vision of the drawing had the Sasq'ets merging with

the trees, the waters, the mountains, and the rocks. The being was seen and unseen depending on the angle the drawing was viewed from. The haunting beauty was more profound than any portrait Leanne had ever conceived. The thought or idea of Sasq'ets brought her to an understanding of home that had previously been foreign to her.

As Leanne cautiously made her way back down the mountain, she reflected on the idea of interconnectedness in a way she had never comprehended before. The idea that people are all one had kind of been a part of her consciousness, but now she felt the truth of that to the very core of her being. She could not contain her enthusiasm to create the drawing, so she began sketching as soon as she got back to her van. By daybreak, she had most of her idea on canvas and then used the light of the sun to refine the picture. It was transformational. She succeeded in capturing the essence of the Sasq'ets, making it appear both seen and unseen. It was truly a master genius creation. And through every stroke, something new was awakening in Leanne. She was seeing, feeling, and sensing on a new and different level. She wept with the joy of arriving to a place of home that she did not know existed or had even missed. Home was there, all the time...waiting within.

Tiny Home

The "Itsy Bitsy Teenie Weenie Yellow Polka Dot Bikini" song was going around and around in Susan's head as she reflected on their tiny home one balmy Saturday afternoon. Even now, it was strange to her that after years of living in a large home with attached garage on seven acres, she and her partner, Barry, could now be content in this small — well, actually tiny — travel home. Downsizing was simplifying life more than they could have imagined. Somehow the RV had become a fit for them at this chapter of their lives. After all, what do people really need in their homes?

The efficient little space had a combined kitchen, dining, and living room, a bedroom, bathroom, washer and dryer, and of course, the great outdoor space. The location they were currently enjoying was in a lovely oceanside development with a good amenities building featuring a fitness room, a salt water pool, and common area for visiting, reading, or classes. There was the sea walk with breathtaking views. Shopping, coffee shops, and restaurants were all within walking distance. Susan was grateful she had the courage to let go of the security of her old life and create something new and, in the process, take herself way out of her comfort zone...

Susan and her partner, Barry, had sold their home and belongings and had purchased an RV ten years prior. They were able to finance this new way of life through travel writing and money saved and earned through the sale of their property. They were both very green in regards to RV travel but had decided to embrace this venture with enthusiasm and open minds and hearts. Their motor home was cozy and comfortable, so it accommodated their reduced needs adequately. They towed a small car so they could get around easily and explore the backroads and hidden gems of the area where they set up their RV.

Getting along in their confined quarters took some time. They needed to learn how to give each other space and to become more tolerant of each other's idiosyncrasies. It took some doing for both of them, but they forged through the many up-too-close-and-personal moments and were grateful for simple distractions, like passing a funky van, glimpses of the sea, pausing at a taco stand, tumbling tumbleweeds, or noticing license plates. It all served to break the tension and monotony of some strained moments on the road.

Their travels took them from landlocked Alberta in Canada, to the windy roads with many "topes" in Baja, California. Experiencing ocean swimming was a new education and challenge and was approached with caution after Susan found herself in a rough wave that sucked part of her swimming suit off. They had a good laugh once the suit was back on and while she searched for it.

The ferry from La Paz on the Baja to Topolobampo and Los Mochis in Mexico cost $770 US — a cash-only purchase — and landed them on mainland Mexico at midnight, which they found out wasn't the ideal time to be out and about. After an exchange with the Mexican police, they were relieved to pull into a shopping center parking lot for the remainder of the night. Thumbing through the Spanish-English dictionary was met with limited results Susan and Barry realized. They would have been better off learning the language of the locals well before embarking on their journey. Still, throughout their travels in Mexico, they came to have a great appreciation of the daily beach buskers in their white clothing and big smiles, the fresh salsa and tacos with the local Tecate beer, and the general kindness of the people.

They hiked at Chiricahua National Monument in Arizona, experiencing the stunning rock formations. The river walk at San Antonio and the ocean walk at the barrier islands of South Padre were just two of many stops in the vast state of Texas. Experiencing those ruby-red grapefruits and fresh pecans were simply delicious in the Rio Grande Valley. Stopping at Dirty Al's for fresh shrimp turned out to be much better than the name implied, and coming upon White Sands National Monument by Alamogordo in New Mexico transported Susan and Barry to another world.

The fields upon fields of produce and the orchards and vineyards in Arizona and California brought a great appreciation for the freshness of food in their lives. Tasting olives and walnuts at the Old Temecula farmers' market and viewing the stunning bouquets of fresh flowers was lovely. Feeling like they were truly walking on holy ground at Tuacahn in Utah and experiencing blue-green like never before at Lake Tahoe in Nevada were both unforgettable memories. And then there were the beaches — oh, the beaches of Oregon, a place to surrender and cry and renew. Walking for miles and discovering agate treasures along the way and stopping for clam chowder with a live sea lion show was so satisfying. The tip of the Sonoran Desert at Osoyoos, BC, showcased a rugged beauty with a summer heat that warmed right to the bone, while kayaking on the Upper Arrow Lake at Nakusp brought a new level of soul connection. Swimming in the mineral-rich waters of Little Manitou in Saskatchewan was a welcomed relief to aching muscles, and Jasper National Park in Alberta brought the sleep that only fresh mountain air can deliver. Childhood memories were triggered when coming upon a true gem — the town of Ladysmith all lit up for Christmas. The peaceful beauty of

HOME

Vancouver Island brought even more awareness to Susan about what home meant for her...

Windswept beaches with sand dollar shells
Grottos and churches with ringing ancient bells
Tomatoes, avocados, peppers, lemons, and limes
Almonds, dates, orange groves, Bougainvillea vines
Abundance showing at every twist and turn
Route maps, interstates — all fun to learn
Best bakery and coffee shops, best fish and chips
Best farmers' markets, best barbecue and dips
Purple desert sunsets and starry Borrego nights
Sedona sunrise — oh, and, yes, Las Vegas lights
The mighty saguaro standing guard over all
Soaring Swainson's hawks, eagles' screeching calls
Cascading crystal clear Kootenay waters
Barking sea lions and curious otters
Tumultuous waves crashing on shore
Aurora borealis humbling to the core
Giant redwoods and cedars and spruce abound
Dwarfing humans and fairy gardens on the ground
Enterprising artisans, busking their wares
Fur babies with humans out getting fresh air
Creating gratitude and a presence of well-being
Contentment and peace and sixth-sense seeing
Wondering and sensing the question of home
Feeling the gypsy and the courage to roam

The wind whipping up the surf and rattling the awning snapped Susan out of her reverie. There was much to reflect on and much to smile and laugh about. She recalled Barry half-heartedly joining her at a sunrise Thai chi class only for him to discover it was a total fit for him. Somehow, for Barry, participating in the slow gentle movements brought forth calmness for him in his daily life. What a treat for Susan to not have to constantly be aware of where his hyper energy was taking them daily. He relaxed — totally relaxed. An additional benefit Barry discovered was that Susan was much more receptive to him since his approach was so calm, often with a dose of humour. *Where did that funny man come from?* Susan found herself pondering at times.

Barry had been very driven and work-directed when he and Susan got together. Time for play hadn't really been a part of Barry's life as, for the most part, work was play for him. And that was a great space to be in. However, his body was giving him signs that he needed change. He had relentless back issues and debilitating headaches. When Susan and Barry embraced the opportunity for change, it wasn't without some trepidation, but curiosity won the day, and they embarked on what turned out to be a fun life adventure. And throughout their travels, a common theme played out in every region, from the mountains to the desert to the sea. It seemed that for the most part, people do wake up in the morning with the desire for a good cup of coffee or tea, harmony with their family and coworkers, working or playing at jobs that are satisfying, and loving kindness for one another. This awareness is contrary to a lot of news and television viewed on a daily basis. There was a definitive difference in people's opinions depending on where they got their daily news. Susan and Barry both made a conscious effort to be aware of what daily babble they were participating in and listening to. They came to recognize the effect of dramatic, negative news on their physiology and so endeavoured to approach daily living with the glass-half-full philosophy. This approach brought a new life and career for Barry. He spent a lot of his time traveling to various retreat centres offering Thai chi and meditation. Susan participated as well, and it became a source of inspiration for her travel writing.

Barry and Susan had become adaptable. The realization that the more they were attached, the less they were connected, became a part of their awareness. Their ability to be "home" wherever they arrived was something they could not have anticipated when embarking on life in a tiny travel home, but it truly was the great reward.

Homemade

"Pistachio! I love pistachios!" That was Wally's reaction to his little nephew Eddy's invitation to try the delectable-looking green dessert featured on the Christmas buffet table. The creamy confection was popular, so the tray was already half empty. Wally dished up generous portions for Eddy and himself and proceeded to gobble it up with Eddy gobbling his at the same time. Wally's smile was huge as he made a show of it for the little guy. Eddy was staring fixedly at his uncle as a competition ensued between the two of them. Wally timed his last bite to coincide with Eddy's so it could be considered a draw or tie. The little guy insisted he swallowed his last bite first so Wally agreed, which meant Eddy got to pick the next game they would play — tag outside.

The family get-togethers were few and far between with distance and schedules becoming a major factor. The days of home-cooking Sunday gatherings seemed like a long time ago now. As Wally reflected on those days gone by, he felt deeply the nostalgia for what had once been: the grandparents holding the space, neutralizing the talk; the uncles arguing politics and religion or talking farming and hunting; the aunties' non-stop conversations interspersed with contagious laughter; the cousins playing, teasing, running, jumping, and of course eating — oh, and the food.

Chicken soup with homemade noodles,
warm buns and poppy seed strudel.
Spätzle with sausage and sauerkraut,
pickled pigs' feet, a favourite no doubt,
Carrot dumplings with beef stew,
a super-secret, never-tell, homebrew
Pies with rhubarb or pumpkin or raisin,
Pierogies with potato and cheddar and bacon
Bison lasagna with garlic toast,
or new potatoes simmering with the pot roast
Sautéed onions with green beans,
Oil-vinegar dressing on fresh salad greens
Cookies maybe ginger, oatmeal, or chocolate chip,
assorted fresh veggies with creamy dips
Everybody's favourite turkey with dressing,
so much gratitude for sweet family blessings

Wally had always been comfortable in his own skin and attributed that to the solid family upbringing he had experienced. He was free to create and explore, however, there were actual rules and consequences when he grew up. His free spirit became quite challenged by the confines and limitations, so he left the area and began his journey of discovery.

For the next fifteen years, Wally created many friendships and connections. His music and street busking net him enough revenue to carry him forward. He had fallen in love a few times over the years, and although he had never fallen out of love, his partners had, so he disciplined himself enough to release them freely. Somehow, he simply could not commit. His soul longed to wander so the very idea of settling down, of remaining in one place, brought a weight on him that he just couldn't bear. Feeling the heartbreak of that decision did inspire him with music. He wrote and performed three particularly haunting and heartfelt songs, which pivoted his music into the spotlight and ultimately got him a record contract. But even the record contract felt confining to Wally. He persevered through, however, and found himself on the touring circuit. He felt most comfortable when they were touring with the bus. There was a stability to returning to the bus after each show as opposed to a hotel room. When they were out of the country, flying from venue to venue, checking in and out of hotel rooms, he felt himself scattering. Trying to keep his body in balance during those shows was a difficult challenge. Trying to either stay awake or go to sleep created a path for different forms of substance abuse. Increasingly, Wally found himself questioning his path.

A word came into his life at this time that created an unsettled feeling within him. That word was *busy*. Busy. He found himself constantly saying that word.

I am busy. I am too busy. I will be busy then. Perhaps another time, I am busy. That will need to be rescheduled as I am busy. It truly began to rattle his cage. He needed to learn to calm his mind, not using alcohol, pot, or drugs. Wally paused and embarked on a new path. It began with bicycling — something he hadn't done since his childhood. As he bicycled for miles, he began to remember things. The smells along the trails awakened and stirred him. *Homemade* came to his mind. Homemade. He was homemade.

Somehow that thought inspired his creativity, and the bicycling stimulated him physically, creating balance within him. Wally created peak fitness physically and emotionally through his miles on the bicycle. The desire for unhealthy substances was replaced with inspiration. His music flourished, as did he. The songs almost tumbled out of him now with his new beat trending as motivating and uplifting. The feedback further lifted him. He was inspired by people's stories about how his music was getting them off the couch and getting outside. Wally became so moved by these stories that the thought came to him about making more bicycles available to those unable to purchase their own. He partnered with a bicycle shop that sold new and also repaired used bicycles. They created a program through volunteering to distribute the bicycles. The murky troubling path was gone and was replaced with a new measure of peace and prosperity and vision.

Wally grinned at Eddy as they went back inside after an hour of building snow forts and snow angels. It was refreshing to be with the little guy. Somehow, it made life simpler and more fun. Wally knew it was time to be home for Christmas as he hadn't been back in ten years. The passage of time was showing itself in both happy and sad ways. His sister's boy, Eddy, now five years old, would be starting school. They were able to catch up in person on four occasions since Eddy was born and tried to connect with FaceTime weekly. Eddy was stuck to Wally like glue since he had arrived for Christmas two days earlier.

Wally's parents were showing age but in a good way. His mom and dad both had careers they enjoyed — his mom, teaching, and his dad, with government. They would be retiring from those jobs in about five years and were planning on doing a lot of gardening, something they shared a love of. Wally thanked them both for making sure he had a music education, which had become pivotal in his life. It was his grandparents who gave Wally the biggest reason to pause. It took his breath away to realize that ten years for them had been a long time. The change in them was dramatic. Grandpa no longer managed on his own and was uncertain of names, places, and days at times. It took him a few minutes of staring at Wally to put a name to him, but when Wally gave his grandpa one of his gentle, real hugs and big grins, he knew his name. And then his grandma was in the hospital on a morphine drip as she prepared for her transition to her heavenly home. Wally sat quietly and held her hand. She squeezed his hand, asking him in a raspy voice about his music and his life. She wanted details, and so he accommodated her. He softly sang parts of the heartbreak songs that had initially set his career on fire. He told her of his loves and losses. She commented on how fit and healthy he looked so Wally shared his story of bicycling and how it brought him home. He shared with her the deep soul satisfaction of volunteering and donating his resources. He thanked her for the many bowls of chicken soup and pieces of pie. He thanked her for all of the times she sewed Halloween costumes for him because he always loved to dress up and she could sew anything. He let her know how fantastic it was that everything was homemade so would be uniquely his own and not replicated. He thanked her for helping him get through his English exams (Grandma was a school teacher, too) and motivating him to finish high school when all he really wanted to do was hit the road.

Grandma understood and felt the deep gratitude from her grandson. She shared with him a final thought that brought tears to his eyes. "You are homemade, Wally."

He received those words from her right to the core of his being. It was what he truly knew. The home he had grown up in remained in him always, to the very fibre of his being, and always would.

Printed in Canada